Growing Readers

For the children
Emma and Paul Rogers

For Oscar
Sophy Williams

VIKING

Published by the Penguin Group
Penguin Books Ltd, 27 Wrights Lane, London W8 5TZ, England
Penguin Books USA Inc., 375 Hudson Street, New York, New York 10014, USA
Penguin Books Australia Ltd, Ringwood, Victoria, Australia
Penguin Books Canada Ltd, 10 Alcorn Avenue, Toronto, Ontario, Canada M4V 3B2
Penguin Books (NZ) Ltd, 182-190 Wairau Road, Auckland 10, New Zealand

Penguin Books Ltd, Registered Offices: Harmondsworth, Middlesex, England

First published 1996
1 3 5 7 9 10 8 6 4 2

Filmset in Goudy

A CIP catalogue record for this book is available from the British Library

ISBN 0–670–86255–X

Printed in Hong Kong by Imago

PAUL AND EMMA ROGERS

CAT'S KITTENS

ILLUSTRATED BY SOPHY WILLIAMS

VIKING

Between two roads, behind a jumble of
buildings, lived Cat and her six kittens.
   Cat had no name because nobody
had given her one.
   Nobody had given her one because
she belonged to nobody.

Cat fended for herself.
She made her own home.
She found her own food.

She fed her kittens, she washed them,
she watched over them while they played.

One starry Sunday night, Cat said to her kittens, "The time will come when you have to fend for yourselves."

So on Monday, the coal-black kitten, the
biggest of the whole litter, went out on his own.
Cat called, "Don't go across the . . .

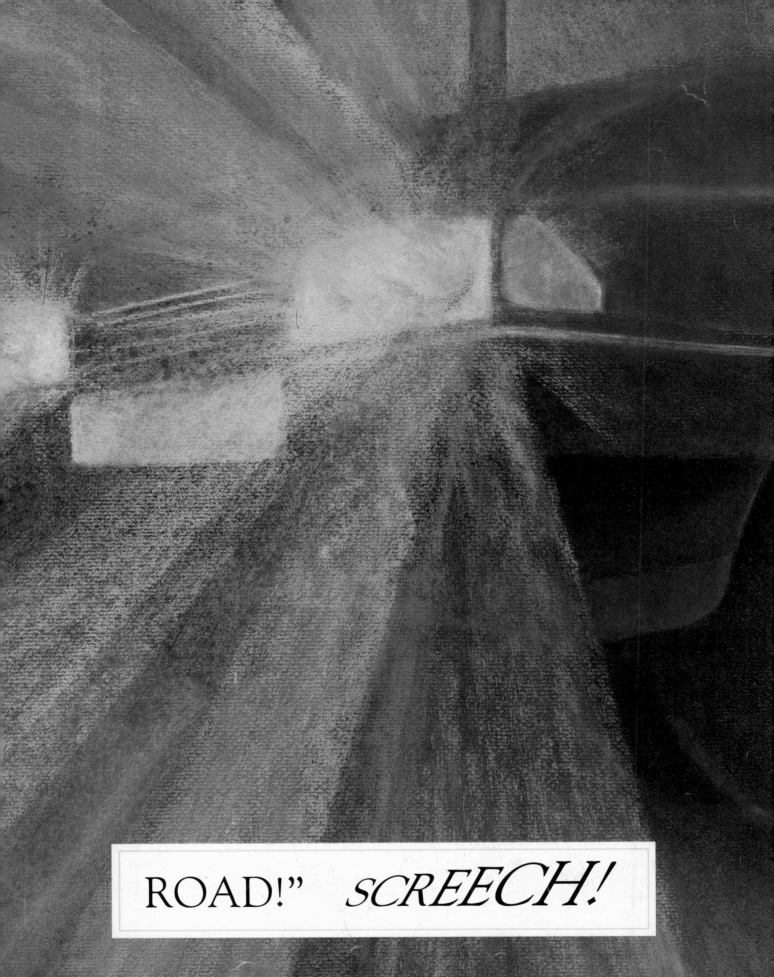

On Tuesday, the ginger kitten went climbing all on her own.

Cat called, "Don't go too far on that . . .

BRANCH!" CRACK!

On Wednesday, the dusty-grey kitten went
sniffing for scraps all on her own.
    Cat called, "Don't fall into that . . .

On Thursday, the brindled kitten went
exploring all on his own.
Cat called, "Don't go near that . . .

DOG!" GRRRRR!

On Friday, the tabby kitten went hunting
all on her own.
Cat called, "Don't take on anything too . . .

BIG!"   SSSSS!

On Saturday, the black kitten and the ginger one, the grey one, the brindled and the tabby all said to the littlest kitten, "It's your turn to go out on your own."

But the littlest kitten snuggled closer to Cat and said, "I'd rather stay here with my mamma."

Sunday night came again and Cat
went out with her kittens.
  They crossed the road.
  They dined at the restaurant.
  They played by the pond.
  They hunted among the bushes.

Then, perched on the wall as the stars began fading, Cat called, "All together now!"

MIAOW!

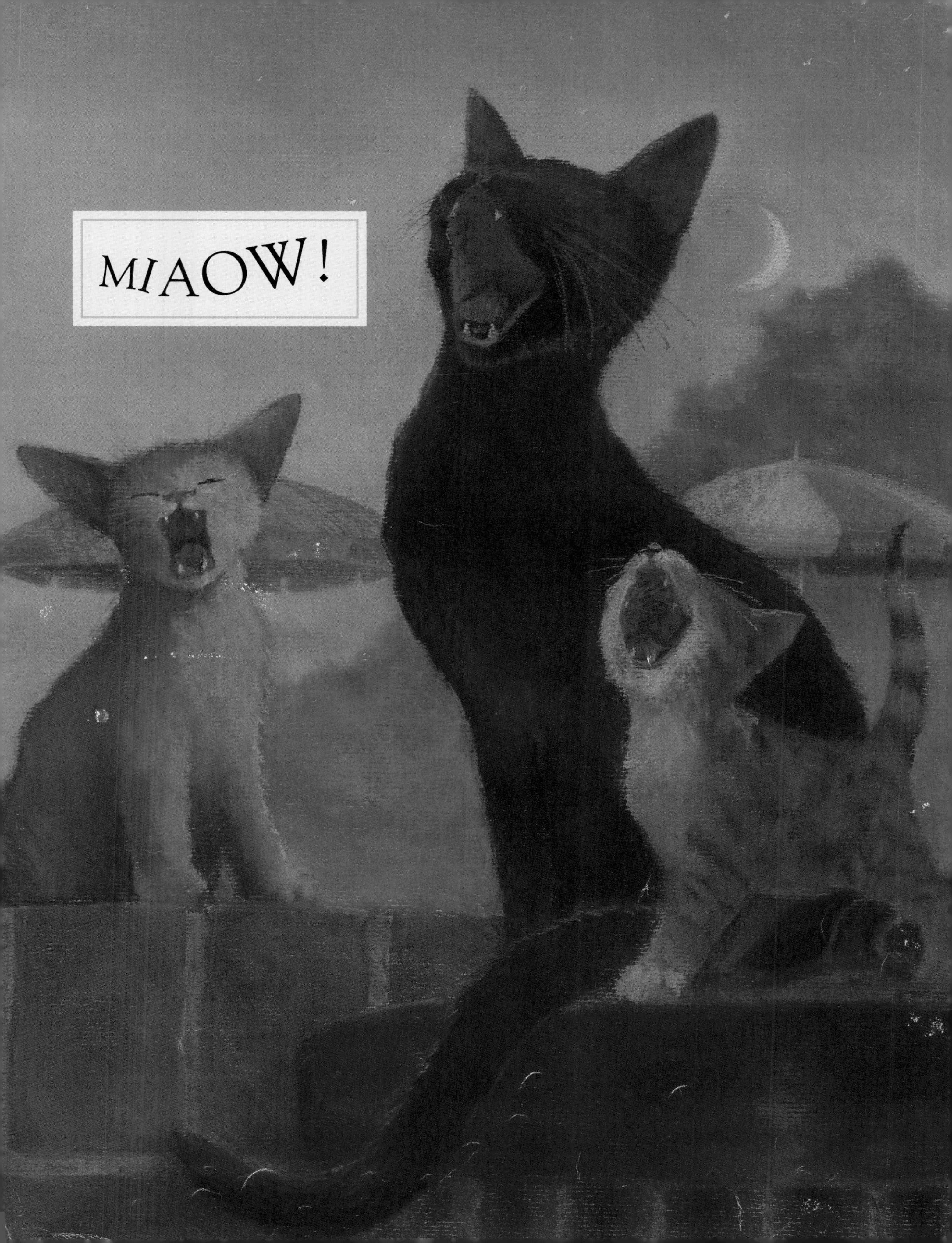

On the way home, Cat told her kittens, "If you want to be city kittens, you have to be careful kittens, you have to be canny kittens."

"Has the time come," asked the littlest one, "the time when we must fend for ourselves?"

"Not yet," said Cat. "Not until your tails are fluffier. Not until your ears are further apart."

Cat's kittens closed their eyes . . .
as tomorrow's sun rose over the city.